JONNA AND THE UNPOSSIBLE MONSTERS

AN ONI PRESS PUBLICATION

JONNA AND THE UNPOSSIBLE MONSTERS

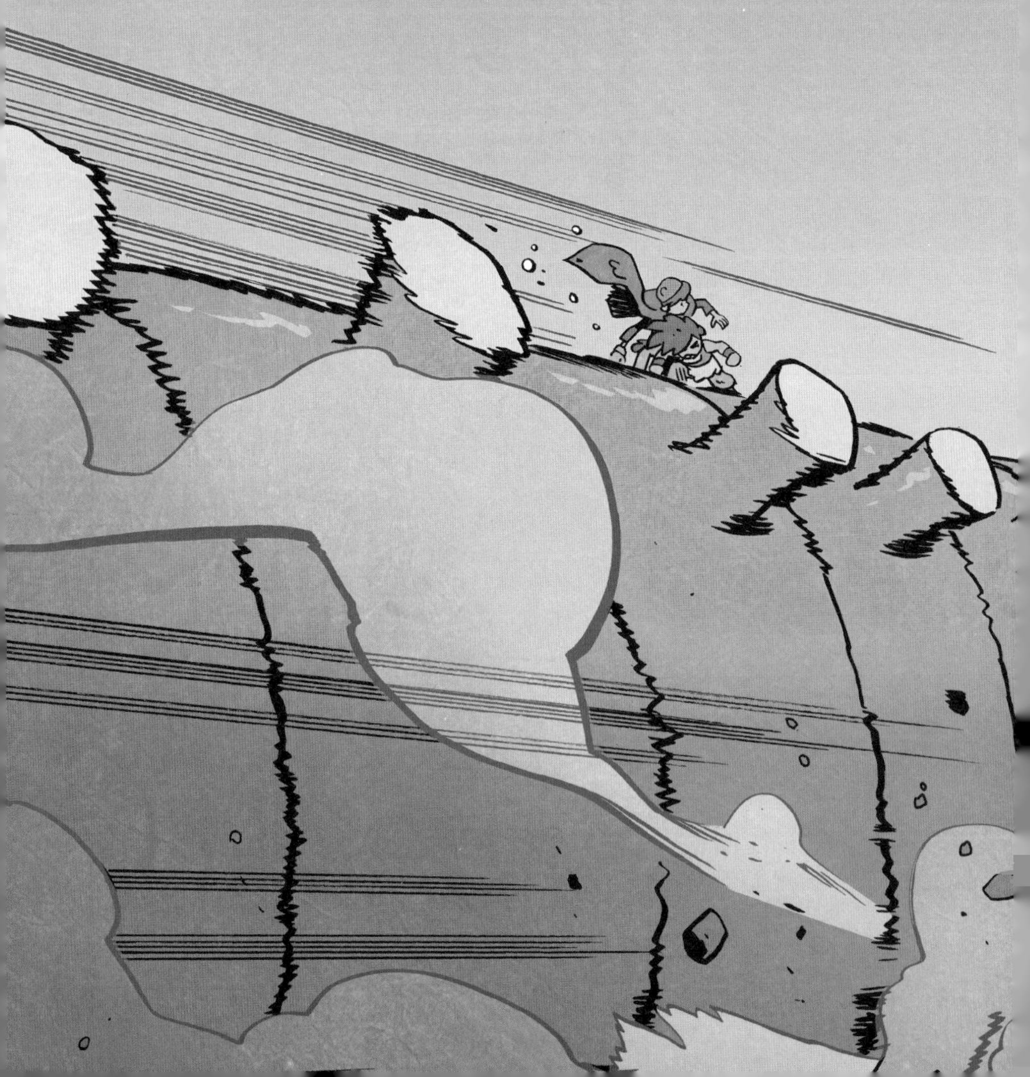

Written by
CHRIS SAMNEE & LAURA SAMNEE

Art by
CHRIS SAMNEE

Colors by
MATTHEW WILSON

Letters by
CRANK! &
CHRIS SAMNEE

Logo Design by RICKY DELUCCO
Book Design by ANGIE KNOWLES with SONJA SYNAK
Edited by ZACK SOTO

Published by Oni-Lion Forge Publishing Group, LLC.

Troy Look, vp of publishing services • Katie Sainz, director of marketing
Angie Knowles, director of design & production • Sarah Rockwell, senior graphic designer
Carey Soucy, senior graphic designer • Chris Cerasi, managing editor
Bess Pallares, senior editor • Grace Scheipeter, senior editor • Gabriel Granillo, editor
Desiree Rodriguez, editor • Zack Soto, editor • Sara Harding, executive assistant
Jung Hu Lee, logistics coordinator & editorial assistant
Kuian Kellum, warehouse assistant

Joe Nozemack, publisher emeritus

onipress.com

@ChrisSamnee | @COLORnMATT | @ccrank

@chrissamnee | @colornmatt | @ccrank

First Edition: May 2023

ISBN 978-1-63715-089-4
eISBN 978-1-63715-109-9

JONNA AND THE UNPOSSIBLE MONSTERS Volume 3, May 2023. Published by Oni-Lion Forge Publishing Group, LLC. 1319 SE Martin Luther King Jr. Blvd., Suite 240, Portland, OR 97214.

Printed in China

Library of Congress Control Number: 2022939572

1 2 3 4 5 6 7 8 9 10

For all the kids who
doodle and daydream

CHAPTER 9

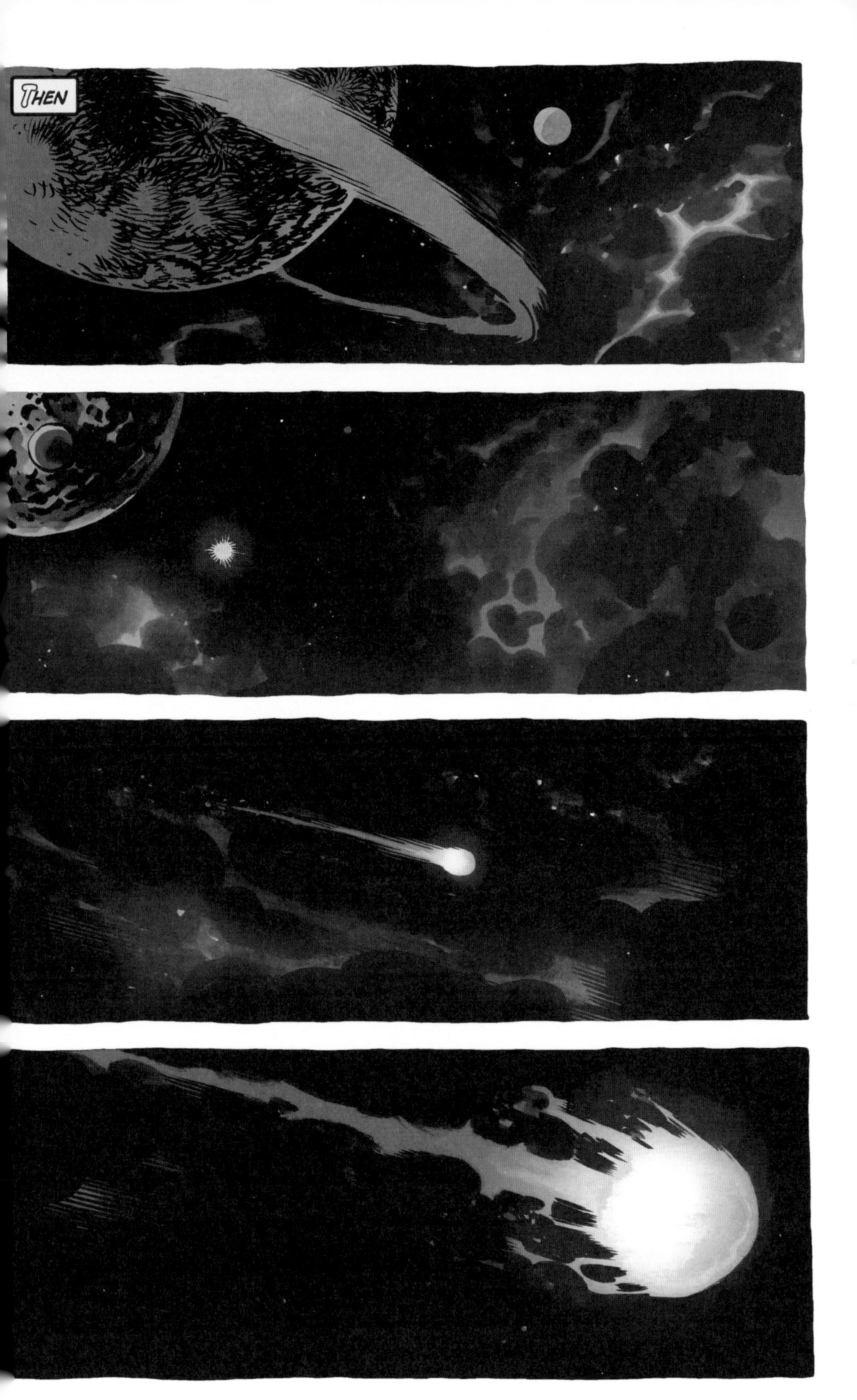
THEN

WHAT IN THE--?
OH NO!!

TINK

PLINK
TAK
TINK

Now
IT...
IT LOOKS JUST LIKE YOU!

IT'S... I'M...

MY SISTER. YOU'RE M SISTER.

NO!

IT'S ME!
STOP!

SNAP

SWIK
SWIK

SOMETHING'S GOT ME!!
LITTLE HELP HERE?
GRRR!
SNAP

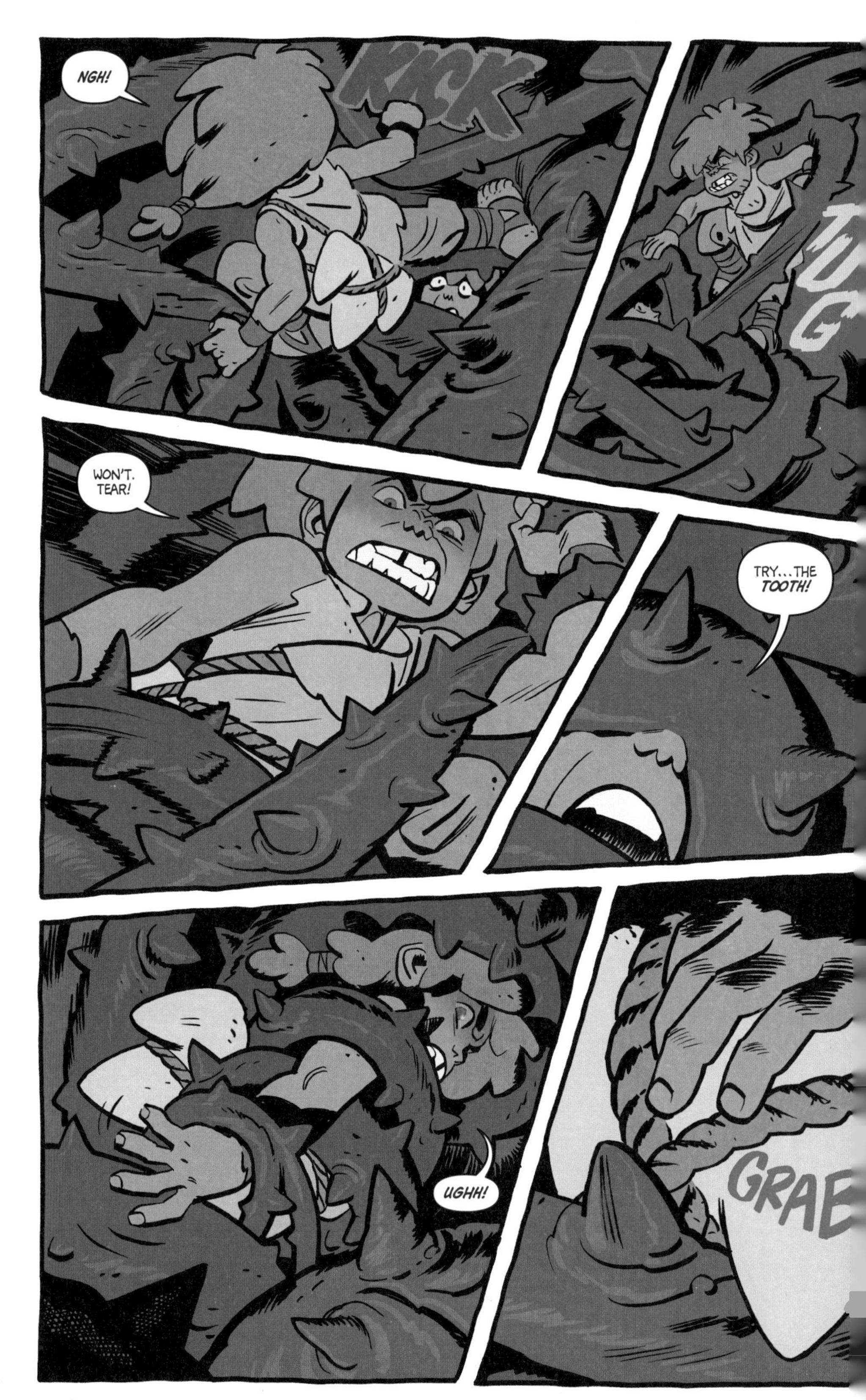
NGH!
KICK
WON'T. TEAR!
TRY...THE *TOOTH!*
UGHH!

UNF!
?!

HF!
HF!
JONNA...
BLINK
I WAS SCARY.
SORRY.
C'MERE.

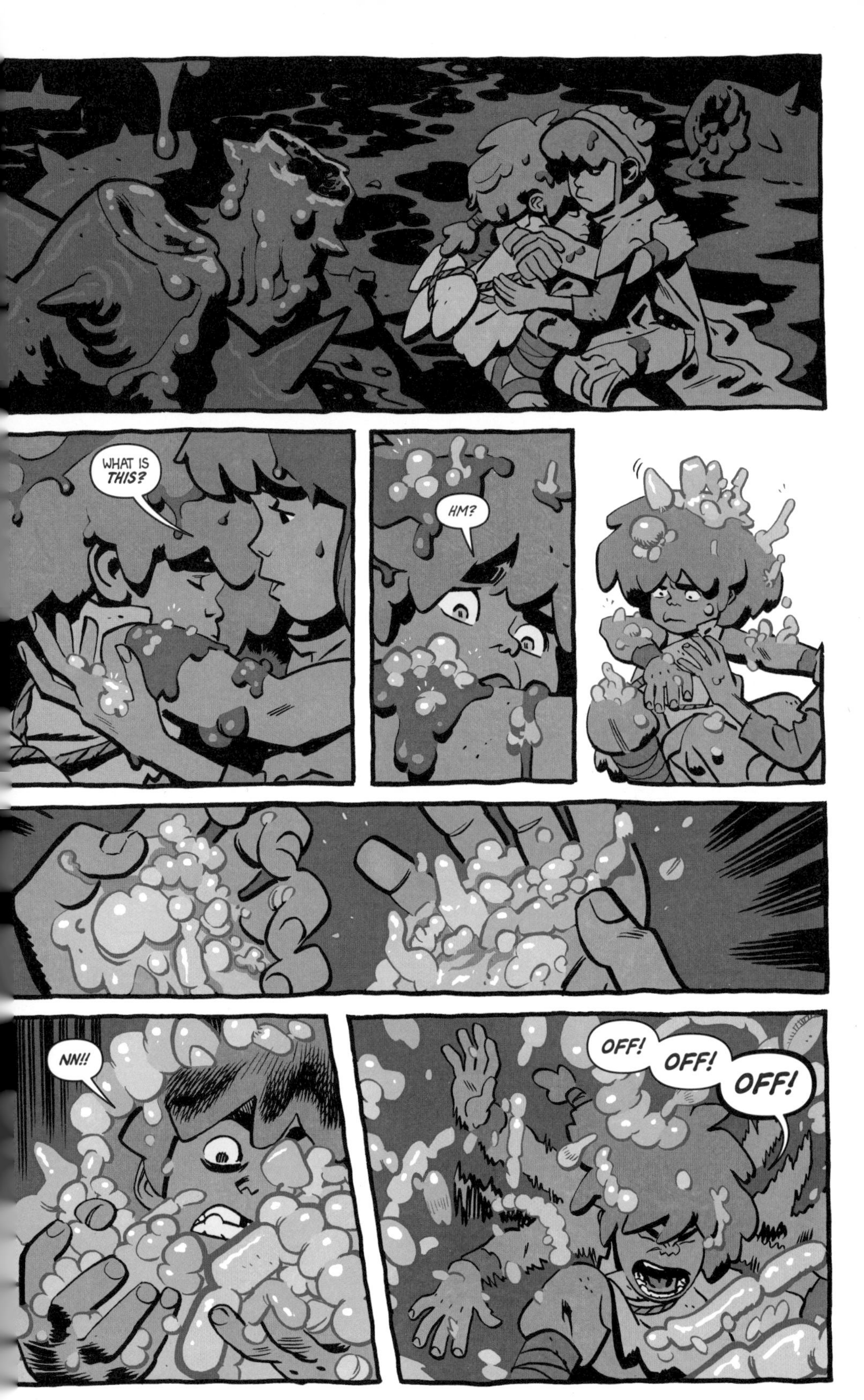
WHAT IS THIS?
HM?
NN!!
OFF!
OFF!
OFF!

HEH.
!!!
HM?
THEY'RE GETTING BIGGER!
AGH! THEY'RE EVERYWHERE!
JONNA!

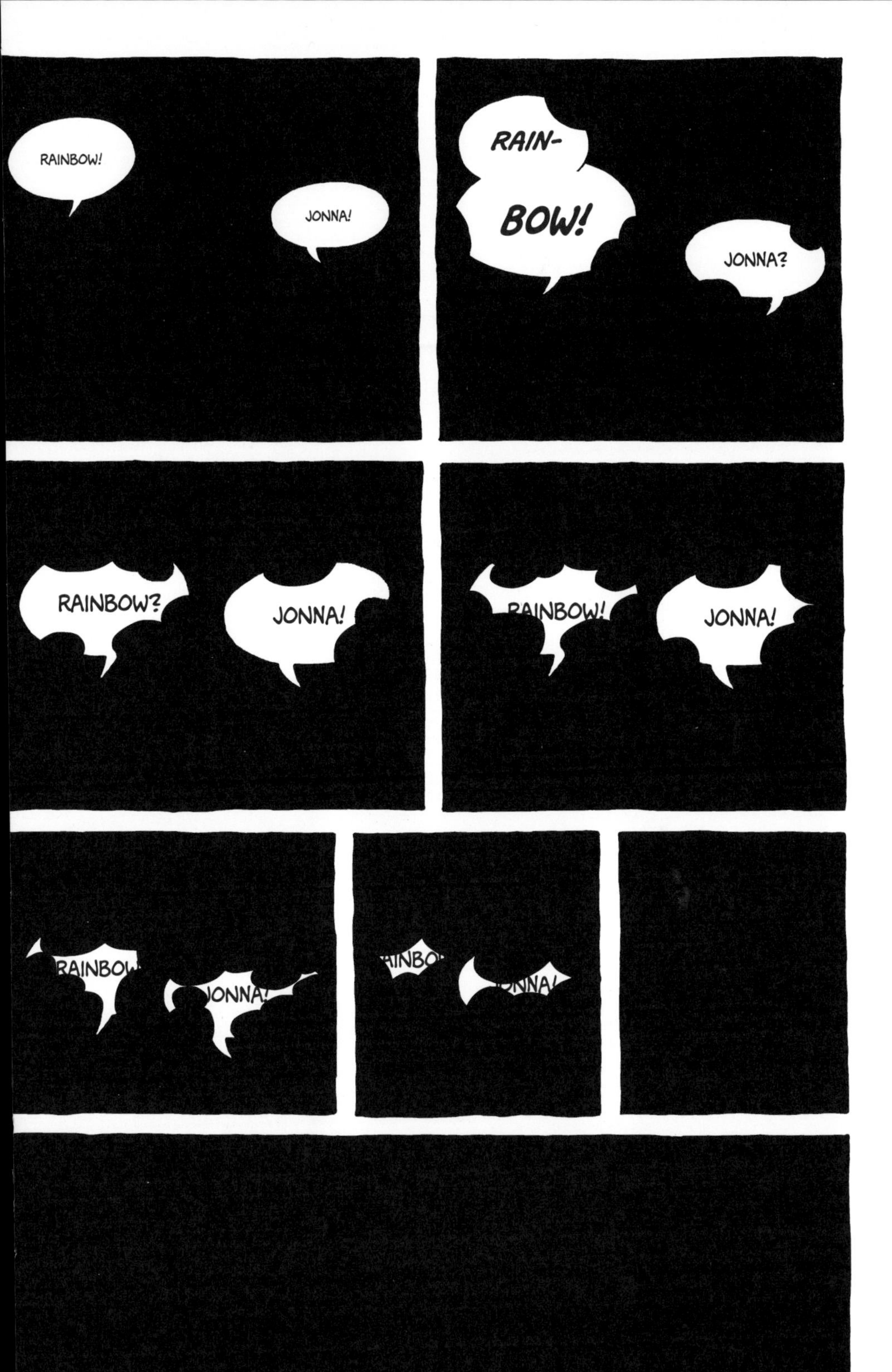

RAINBOW!
JONNA!
RAIN-
BOW!
JONNA?
RAINBOW?
JONNA!
AINBOW!
JONNA!
AINBO
JONNA
INBO
NNA

BLOP
BLORP

MEANWHILE...
KLANK
PANG
KNCH
SLLOIICE

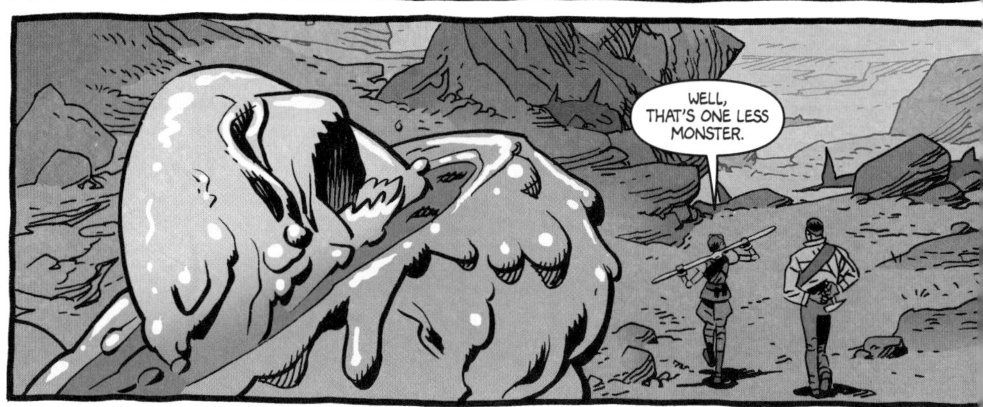
WELL, THAT'S ONE LESS MONSTER.

WE WON'T SEE THAT GUY AGAIN.
NOW WE JUST NEED TO FIND THOSE GIRLS.

UHHHH, NOMI?
NOT NOW. I THINK... IS THAT *THEM?*

IT'S THEM! IT'S THEM!
JONNA?!
GASP!
OH, THANK GOODNESS!
FFBLEH!
HUG
HUG
HUG
?
!!!

CHUG CHUG CHUG CHUG

CHUG

CHAPTER 10

LOOKIT!
WE'RE STILL *ALIVE?!*

WOW!
LOOK AT THAT!

"WOW"?
OH NO, HOLD ON!!

JONNA??
JONNA, WE'RE GONNA...

HM?
OH, THANK
GOODNESS!
ARE
YOU...
OKAY?
OKAY.
LOOK.

EGG.

THOSE MONSTERS ARE GETTING CLOSER!
THINK THERE'S AN OPENING SOMEWHERE ON THIS THING?
J--?
WH--?

NO DOOR!
WE HAVE TO FIGURE SOMETHING OUT QUICK OR WE'RE GONNA GET SMOOSHED!
PANG
HNNGH!
ARE YOU OKAY?

NNGH!
OUCH.
CAN YOU FIGHT?
MAYBE?
KRK
KRRK
THAT'S OKAY-- WE'LL FIGURE SOMETHING OUT.

NO.
BACK.
?

GET BACK!
HUH?!
WHAT?!

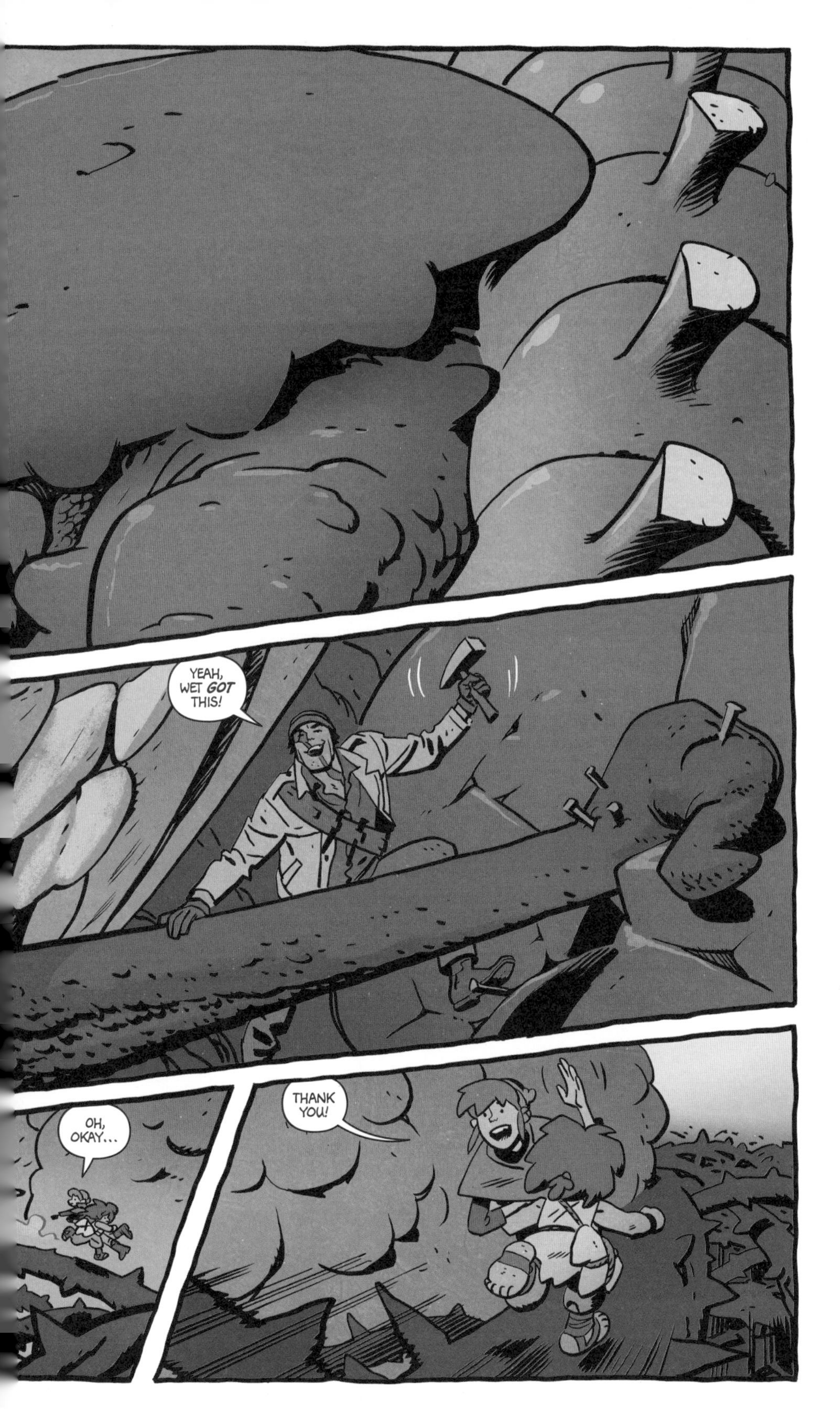
YEAH, WET GOT THIS!
OH, OKAY...
THANK YOU!

WHEW! NOW I CAN THINK FOR A SEC--
UM...

OH, COME ON!!

BLOOSH!
FWAP
I GOTCHA. C'MON.
GET--

OFFA ME!!!
OH.
HEH!
HAHAHA!
HAHA!

WAY TO GO, YOU!
FLEX
DO WE GO BACK AROUND? OR GO IN?
IN! IN!!

CHAPTER 11

JONNA, NO. YOU SAID YOU CAN'T TAKE ON *TWO*, RIGHT?!
WE DON'T STAND A CHANCE AGAINST *ALL* OF THESE!
NO. GOTTA FIGHT.

JONNA, NO!
STOP!
GRRR!
FINE!
SWAPT
!
SSSPLUURPPT

OKAYYY, NOT WHAT I WAS EXPECTING.

NGH!

SOMEBODY...
...IN MY HEAD...
DAD!
?
C'MON!
DID-- DID YOU SAY "DAD"?!

OHHHH...

STOP IT!
WHATEVER YOU'RE DOING IS HURTING HER!!
IN HERE?
D-DAD?!
NO, I'M NO FATHER OF YOURS.
THE LITTLE ONE, THOUGH...

SHE'S ONE OF MINE--
YOU'RE HERE TO HELP ME MAKE SOME USE OF THIS WORTHLESS PLANET.
YOU BELONG TO ME--MORE THAN THIS SACK OF MEAT I'M SPEAKING THROUGH.
NO WAY. I--
I'M NO EGG MANSTER.
AND YET YOU ARE PART OF ME. CONNECTED BY--
RUN, GIRLS! RUN!
GET OUT WHILE YOU CAN!!
UNFF!

--CONNECTED BY AN INVISIBLE VINE.

ALL OF MY CHILDREN ARE.

TO PUT DOWN ROOTS--

WHEN I LEFT MY PLANET--

AND CAME HERE--

MY CHILDREN HELPED TILL THE SOIL, TAMP DOWN RESISTANCE, MAKE THE ATMOSPHERE MORE DIFFICULT FOR SURVIVAL.

YOU ARE THE FIRST OF YOUR KIND. INTENDED TO BLEND IN WITH THESE ANTS AN DESTROY THEM FROM THE GROUND--BUT SOMETHING WEN WRONG.

THE PLAN WAS THE SAME AS ALWAYS.
TO ABSORB ALL THEIR RESOURCES AND MOVE ON.
BUT ROOTS ARE NOT ENOUGH.
NO! SHE'S *NOT* ONE OF YOU--
NO, SHE'S NOT. YOU'VE RUINED HER FOR ME.
AN ORPHAN OF TWO SPECIES-- AND A MONSTER TO BOTH.
I AM NOT A MONSTER!!

YOU'LL... ALWAYS BE... MY LITTLE G--
ENOUGH!!
DAD!!
ONCE, I WAS JUST A POD, FEASTING ON A SMALL PLANET.
BUT AS I GREW, I NEEDED MORE ENERGY TO SUSTAIN MYSELF.

I LOVE Y--

NO WAY--
SILENCE. THE PROCESS IS NEARLY COMPL--
I'LL SHOW YOU...
I THINK WE REALLY TICKED IT OFF.

NO!
WAY!!!

YOUR ADOPTED PEOPLE-- THIS PLANET--ARE NOTHING BUT A RESOURCE.
FUEL. AND THEIR USEFULNESS HAS COME TO AN END.

JONNA, YOU CAN'T...
I CAN. I *CAN.*
JONNA! ***UGGHHH!!***
GRAAAAAH--
OH NO!
HELP!

GASP!
GET YOU!!

WE'RE ALIVE!
THANK YOU!
YOU THINK YOU CAN SAVE EVERYONE?
OKAY-- GET HIM, JONNA!!

!
DAD!
GOTCHA!

HUNH?!
TH-- THANKS!
DAD! JONNA, FIND DAD!

CHAPTER 12
SAMNEE '22

RAINBOW, STAY BACK.
NO WAY! WE'RE GONNA GET YOU OUT OF THERE!
IT'S STARTING TO DRAG ME DOWN.
I'M TOO WEAK.
I CAN'T--
GO.
GET YOUR SISTER. SAVE YOURSELVES.
NO! WE'LL FIGURE SOMETHING OUT! WE--
Snap

WE CAME HERE TO GET YOU!
WE'RE NOT GONNA--
WAIT--
IT'S PULLING ME DOWN! YOU HAVE TO GO!
JONNA!
JONNA, THE TOOTH! THROW ME THE TOOTH!

HERE.
MISS
NOOOOO!
OH NO, DAD!
THAT WAS MY ONLY IDEA!

CATCH
GOR! NOMI!
HEY, YOU DROP THIS?
NICE WORK, KID. WE GOT IT FROM HERE.
'KAY, THANKS!
CUT CUT
MY GIRLS...
FIGHT ME, FISH HEAD!!

HNNNGG!
GOOM
?!
SWAPT
NICE TRY.
YOUR TINY HANDS CAN'T DO ANYTHING TO ME.
THIS FIGHT IS OVER...
YOU NEVER HAD A CHANCE.

NO WAY!
I WIN!!
WHERE DID--?
I BEAT MONSTERS--
YOU BIG, MEAN MONSTER.

PUNCHING ISN'T DOING ANYTHING! IT'S TOO STRONG!
SHE NEEDS HELP!
JONNA, HOLD ON!
CAN YOU GET HER THE TOOTH??
TOSS
TOGETHER WE CAN!
PLINK

CATCH
CHA!!

KRAK

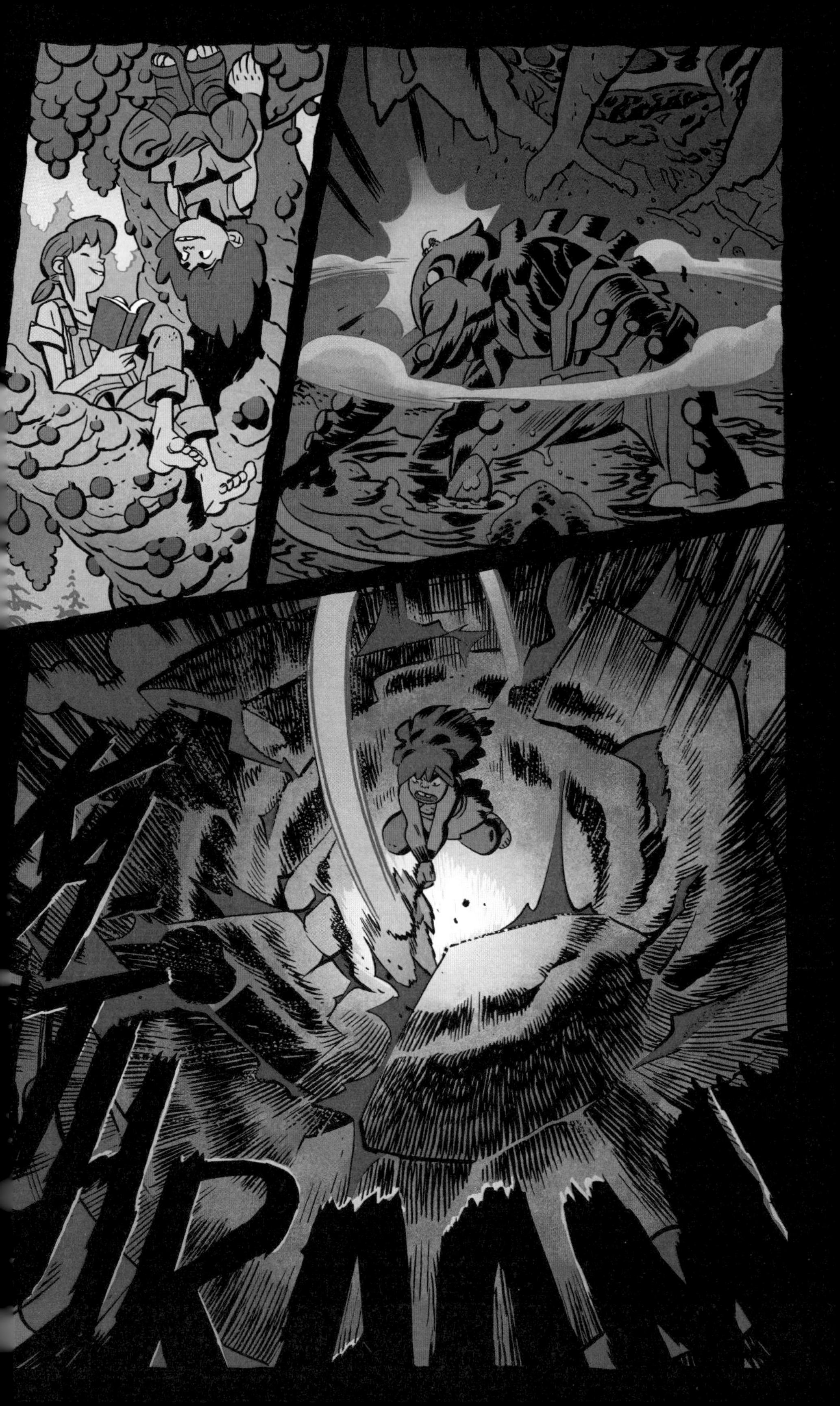

SHE DID IT!
SHE DID IT!!

I WIN!
HE'S TAKING THE WHOLE PLACE DOWN WITH HIM!
WE NEED TO GO!
BUT WHERE'S JONNA?!

FOLLOW THE CURRENT!
IT'S FALLING IN!
JONNA! JONNA!!
WE HAVE TO GO!
NO!

IT'S NOW OR NEVER, FRIENDS!
YOU'RE GONNA GET CRUSHED!
JONNA!
SHE'S STRONG. SHE'LL BE OKAY!
JONNA!!

KRIK
KRRAKK
THERE'S LIGHT UP AHEAD!

KRAKKT
SPFFT
CRUMBLE
OH NO!
LET'S GET THESE FOLKS OUT OF HERE!

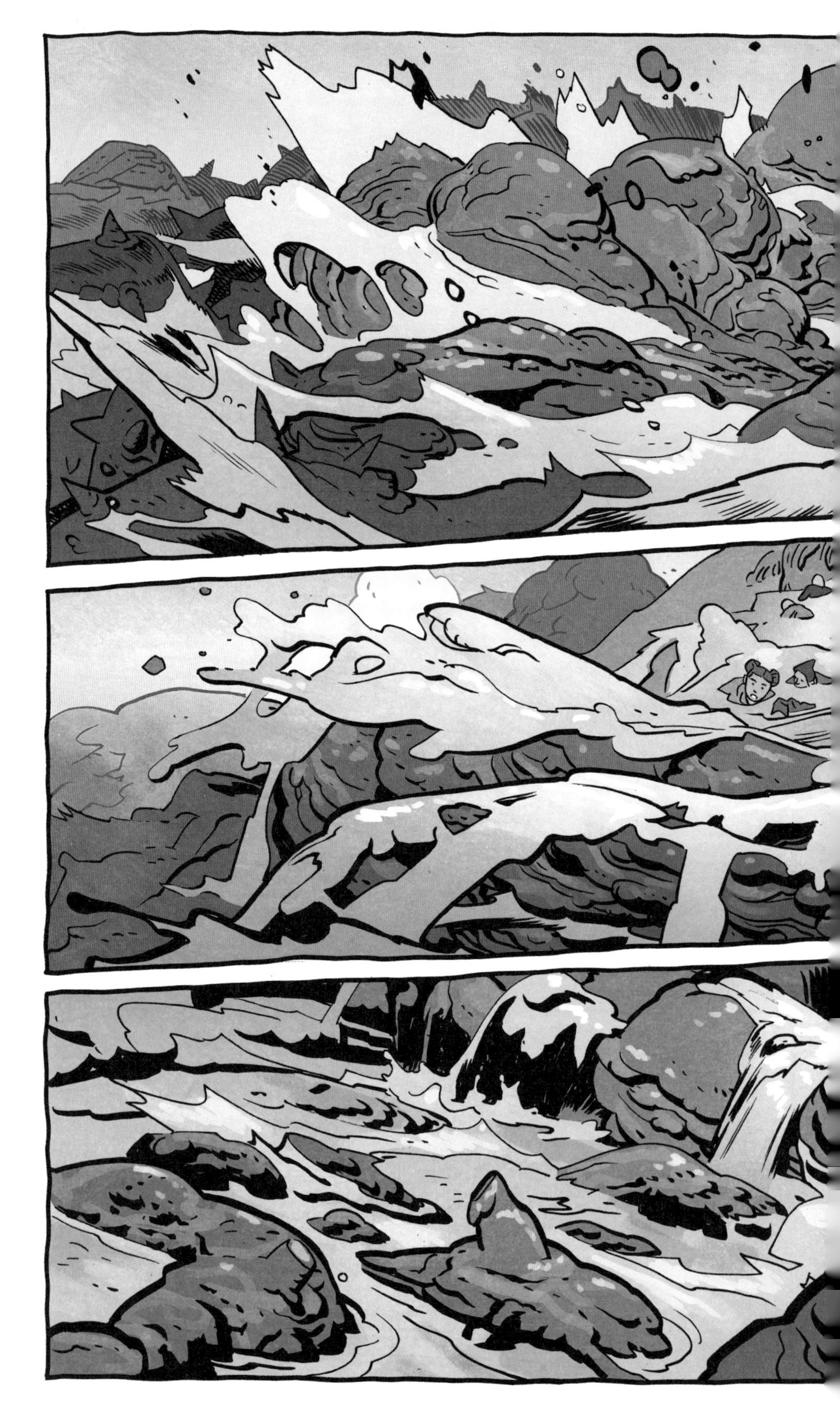

ONE YEAR LATER

OH.
HM?

LUCKIER THAN THE LAST ONE, I HOPE.

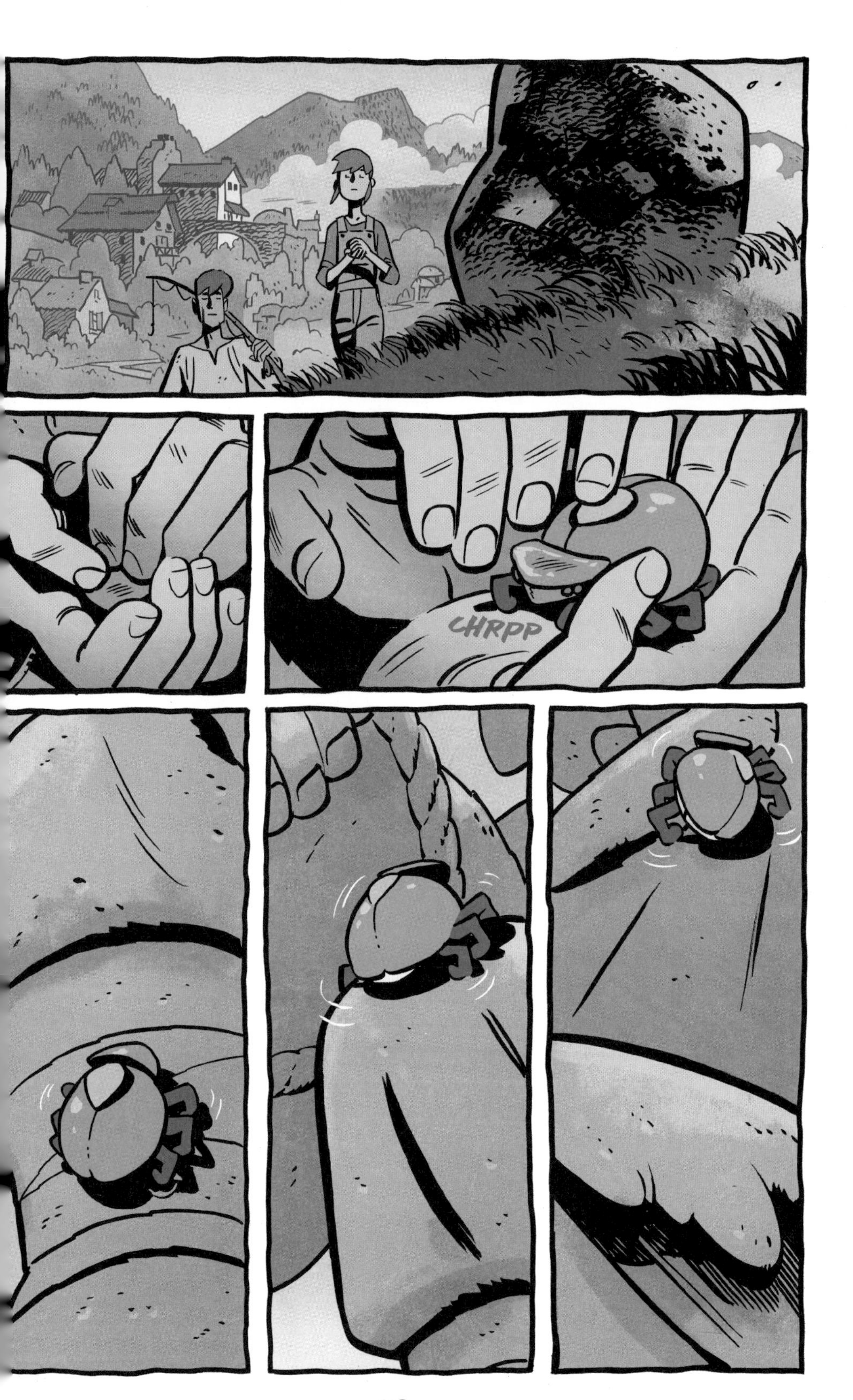

CHRPP

HI, JONNA.
SHE WOULD'VE LIKED THAT BUG.
SHE WOULD HAVE *EATEN* THAT BUG!

I MISS HER.
ME TOO, KIDDO.
PLIP
KRK
TCH
KAK
CHK

JONNA!

WRITTEN BY
CHRIS SAMNEE
&
LAURA SAMNEE

ART BY
CHRIS SAMNEE

COLORS BY
MATTHEW WILSON

LETTERS BY
CRANK!

EDITED BY
ZACK SOTO

THE END

BIOGRAPHIES

CHRIS SAMNEE
is an Eisner and Harvey Award-winning cartoonist.
He's best known for his work on *Daredevil, Black Widow,* and *Thor: The Mighty Avenger*. He lives in St. Louis, Missouri, with his wife, Laura, and their three daughters.

LAURA SAMNEE
lives in St. Louis, Missouri, with her husband, Chris, and their three daughters.

MATTHEW WILSON
has been coloring comics since 2003. He's a two-time Eisner Award winner for Best Coloring and has collaborated with Chris Samnee on more projects than he can recall. When he's not coloring comics he's out on a hike with his wife and two dogs.

CHRISTOPHER CRANK (CRANK!)
has lettered a bunch of books put out by Image, Dark Horse, Oni Press, Dynamite, and elsewhere. He also has a podcast with comic artist Mike Norton and members of Four Star Studios in Chicago (crankcast.com) and makes music (sonomorti.bandcamp.com). Catch him on Twitter: @ccrank and Instagram: ccrank

THANKS FOR READING!

-TEAM JONNA